Rock and Roll

HAZEL TERRY

TINY OWL

High up in the mountains, there were two boulders called Rock and Roll.

One stood flat and one stood tall.

Both sat in awe
and wonder ...

... at the beauty of the world.

Through countless
sunrises and sunsets,

they had blushed and
winked at each other.

They had spent long nights ...

... watching the stars and the universe sparkling above.

They had stood in the
heat of many summers,
admiring the rainbows
in the valley below.

They had endured endless winters of ice, gales, hail, and snow.

Proudly, they wore the badges of the passage of time and the passing of the years.

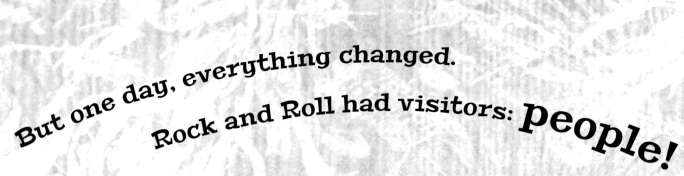

But one day, everything changed.
Rock and Roll had visitors: people!

The boulders were fascinated and tickled pink.

The new visitors
brought gifts for
Rock and Roll.

Flags, cairns, and necklaces
of bunting and rope.

At first, the
boulders loved
these adornments.

But then, they
became jealous
of each other's
new things.

Roll whined to the wind
and said mean things
about Rock and its
colourful wreath of flags.

Rock complained
to a cloud and said
cruel things about
Roll's crown
of stones.

This made the wind
and the cloud unhappy.
They started banging
into each other, arguing
about *their* boulders.

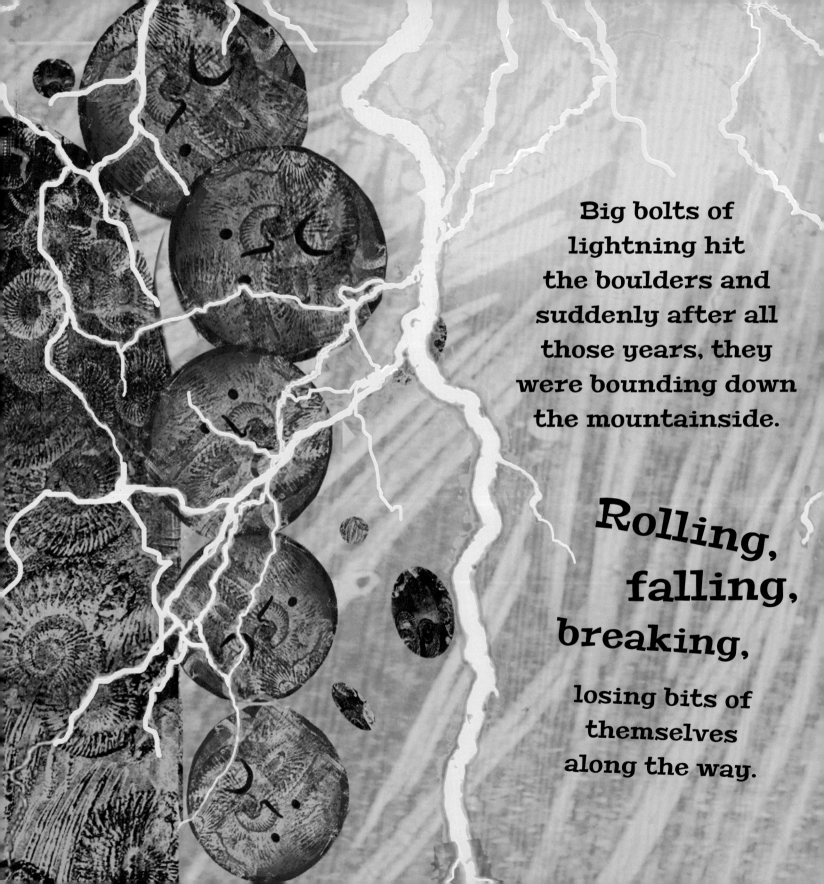

Big bolts of
lightning hit
the boulders and
suddenly after all
those years, they
were bounding down
the mountainside.

Rolling,
falling,
breaking,

losing bits of
themselves
along the way.

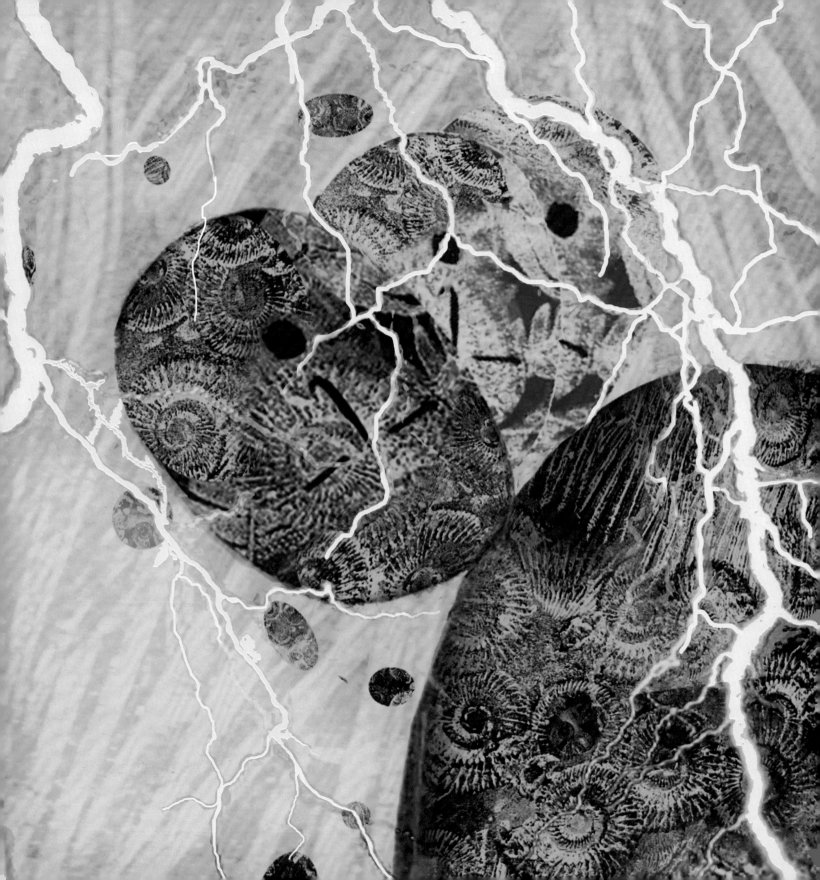

Until, they were no longer big, important boulders on top of vast mountains. They were little pieces of rock, stone, and grit.

And all of the arguments rolled away.

Everyone was happy, and all of the things the boulders had coveted were shared and they were happy together again.

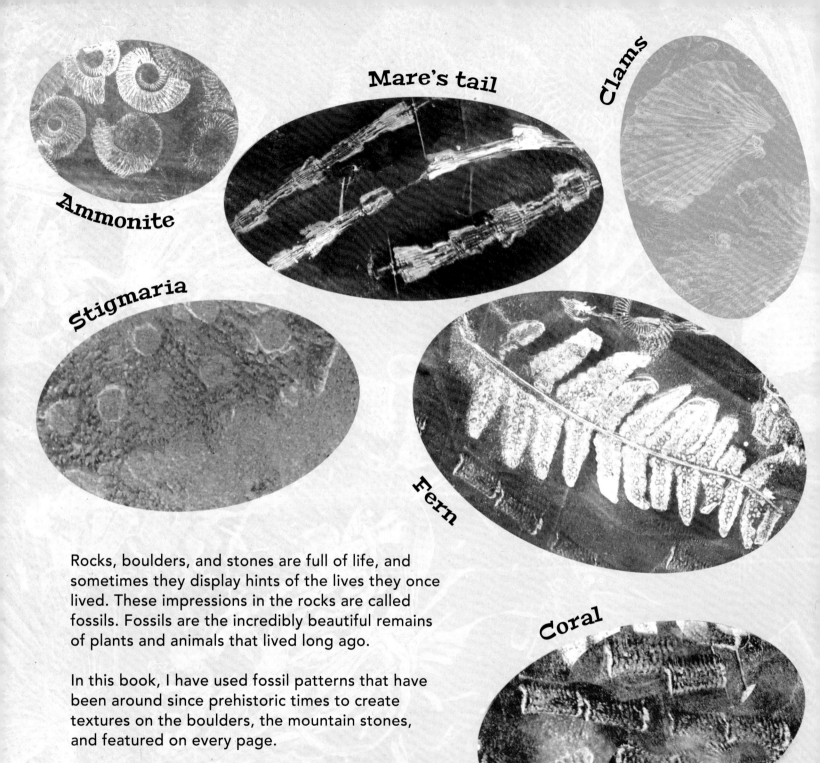

Ammonite

Mare's tail

Clams

Stigmaria

Fern

Coral

Rocks, boulders, and stones are full of life, and sometimes they display hints of the lives they once lived. These impressions in the rocks are called fossils. Fossils are the incredibly beautiful remains of plants and animals that lived long ago.

In this book, I have used fossil patterns that have been around since prehistoric times to create textures on the boulders, the mountain stones, and featured on every page.

I wanted to show that life is all interconnected, precious, and important.